Jennifer Jones

won't Leave Me Alone

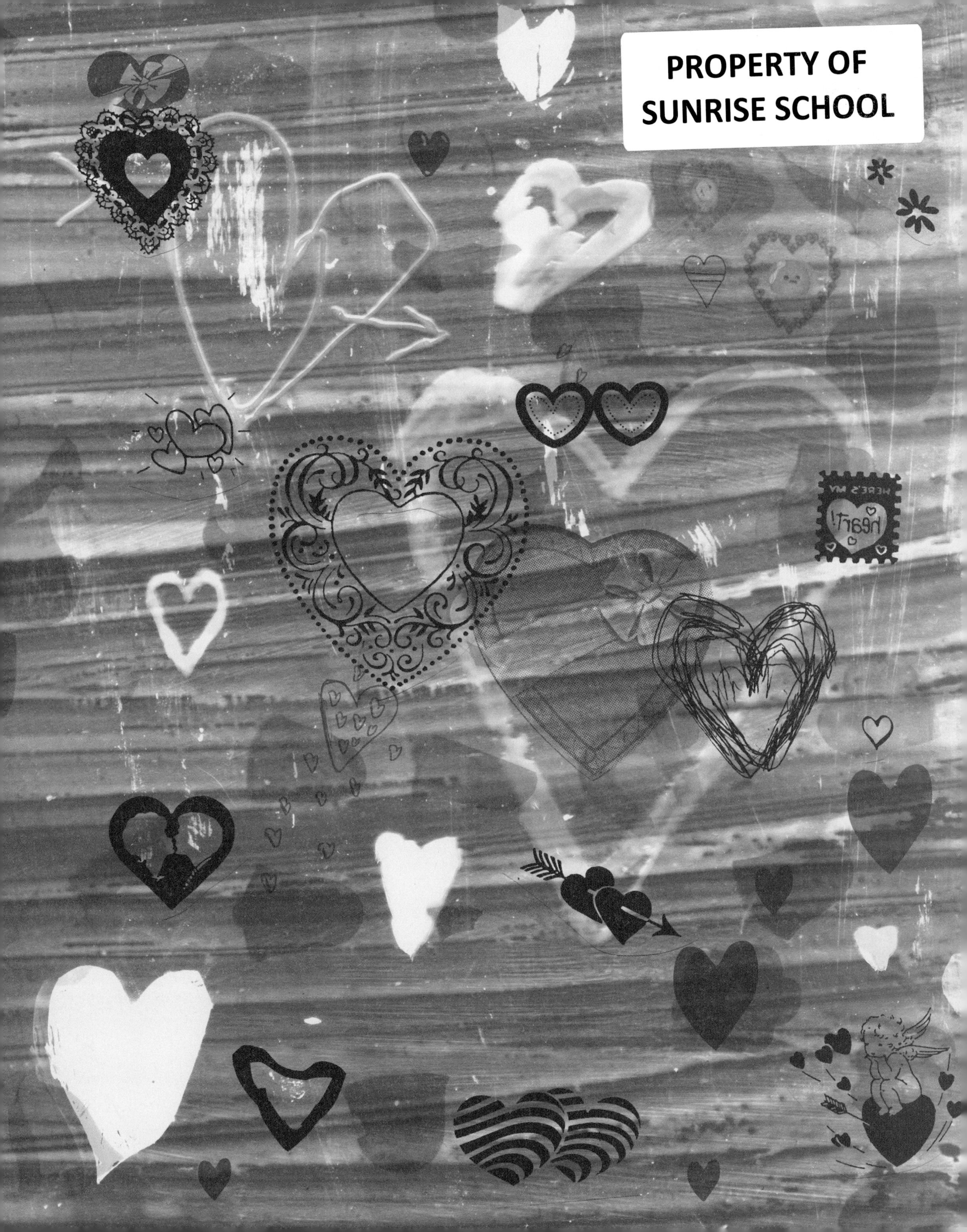

For my friend, Phoebe Gilman
F.W.

For Gabriel and Apple, with thanks to Dr. Hok
N.L.

ISBN 0-439-60317-X

Text copyright © 2003 by Frieda Wishinsky.
Illustrations copyright © 2003 by Neal Layton. All rights reserved.
Published by Scholastic Inc., 557 Broadway, New York, NY 10012,
by arrangement with Carolrhoda Books Inc., a Division of Lerner Publishing Group.
SCHOLASTIC and associated logos are trademarks and/or
registered trademarks of Scholastic Inc.

12 11 10 9 8 7 6 5 4 3 2   4 5 6 7 8 9/0

Printed in the U.S.A.   40

First Scholastic printing, January 2004

Jennifer Jones
won't Leave Me Alone

Frieda wishinsky

Neal Layton

SCHOLASTIC INC.

New York   Toronto   London   Auckland   Sydney
Mexico City   New Delhi   Hong Kong   Buenos Aires

Jennifer Jones won't leave me alone.
She sits by my side.
She **SHOUTS** in my ear.

She tells me she loves me.
She calls me her "dear."

She writes me love poems
Full of words like **adore**,
Then she sticks on red hearts
She bought at the store.

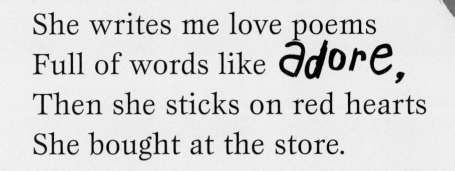

And my friends laugh and snicker.
They point and they stare.
They say,

WELL, WE DON'T AND I HATE IT!

I've had quite enough.
I wish that she'd move
And take all her stuff.

She could move to the jungle
And live in a tree

And talk to the monkeys,
Instead of to me.

But if she insists
That she's not going there,

She could head for the Arctic
And bother a bear.

Or fly to
the desert

Or go to the moon.

I really don't care,
As long as it's soon.

Hip Hip Hooray!

Guess what I heard?
Jennifer's moving.
Her mum's been transferred.

"I'll miss you,"
she said with a
tear in her eye.
Then she gave me
a kiss and whispered,

"Good-bye."

Now her seat is all empty.
There's nobody there.
There's no one to kiss me.

There's no one to care.

So I write in my notebook.
I add and subtract.
I study my spelling.
I learn a new fact.

$$1 + 1 =$$

$$+ 8 =$$

potato

fox

peas

But it's boring! It's lonely!
I miss her a lot.
I wish she'd return

    To her usual spot.

And to make matters worse
She writes, "It's divine
Seeing Paris at night,

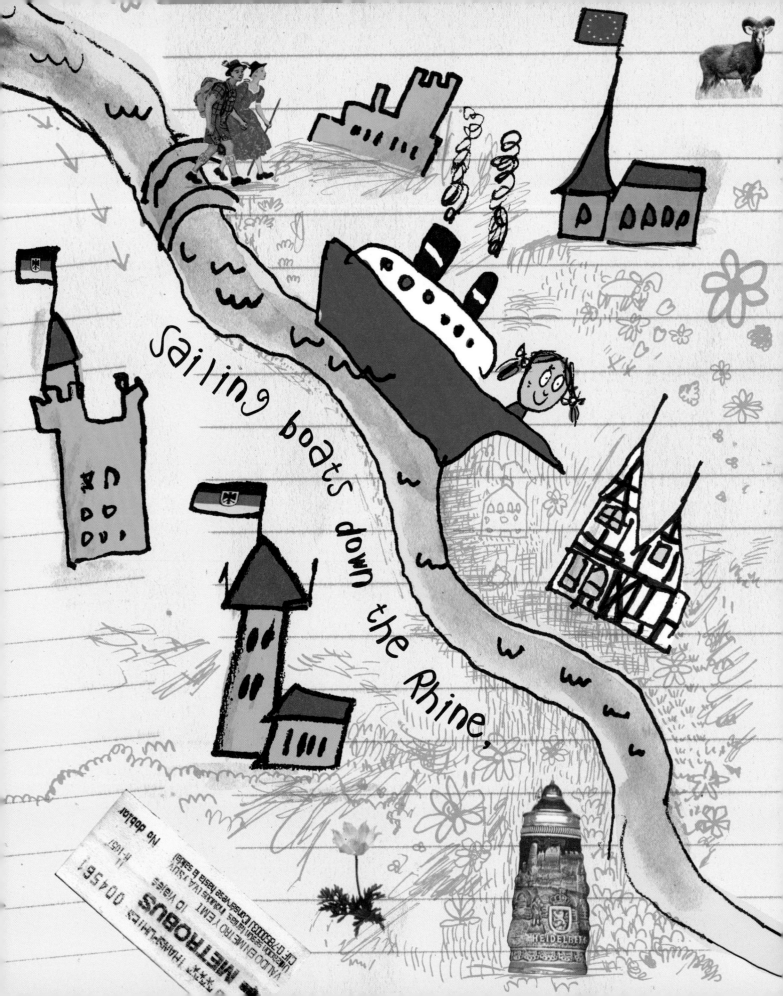

sailing boats down the Rhine,

Munching chocolates in Brussels,

Eating pizza in Rome,

CIAO!

CARTE POSTALE

Miss W. Fish
41 Randolph St.
Cowley Rd.
Oxford

Percy Lubbock,
Emmetts,
Id

"Nibbling viennese pastries you can't get at home."

Percy Lubbock, Esqu

Emmetts

Jennifer's having such fun,
I thought in despair.

She'll never come home.
She'll stay over there.

But then I read on,
"I'll see you in June."
And I yelled,

"WHOOP-DEE-DEE-DOO!!!

She'll return very soon."

And as soon as I did,
The kids wondered why
I was jumping and shouting.
So I thought,

should I lie?

But I told them the truth
As I opened the door.
Then I ran off to buy

Red hearts
at the store.